Gol
and the ......

By Derek Grant and Michael Jones

**Published by
MD Jones Books
mdjones303@outlook.com**

CW00853732

No charge is made for amateur performances anywhere in the world on the basis that a separate copy is bought for each member of the cast.

For Professional Performance Licences, please contact the copyright holder, **mdjones303@outlook.com**

Other scripts available include:

Pantomimes
Little Red Riding Hood
The Adventures of Dick Whittington and his Cat
Humpty Dumpty and the Queen of Hearts
Mother Goose
Goldilocks and the Three Bears
Aladdin

Drama
Treasure Island
The New Adventures of Pinocchio
The Snow Queen
A Christmas Carol

Goldilocks and the Three Bears

Cast of Characters

Goldilocks

Ringmaster

Mummy Bear

Simple Simon

Daddy Bear

Baron Von Lederhosen

Sarah the Cook

Russell the Crow (puppet with voice-over)

Baby Bear (puppet with voice-over)

Sound Cues

Act One
1. Announcement
2. Overture
3. Phone ringing
4. Circus song
5. Baron play-on
6. Baron play-off
7. Baron play-on
8. Grand Old Duke of York
9. Grand Old Duke of York
10. Bears' entrance music
11. Bears' play-off/ Dame entrance
12. Sandwiches and Marmalade
13. Sandwiches and Marmalade
14. Dame play-off
15. Play-off/ mood change
16. Bears' song
17. Bears' rap
18. Bears' song
19. Final chords/ Announcement

Act Two
20. Entr'acte/ Announcement
21. Baron play-on
22. Baron play-off
23. Teddy Bear song
24. Teddy Bear song reprise (tag)
25. Baron play-off
26. Goldie's love song

27. Dame play-on
28. Simon and Dame play-off
29. Mood change
30. Baron play-on
31. Baron play-off (rapid)
32. Bears' rap
33. Circus song (reprise)
34. Finale walk-down
35. Final chords
36. Exit Music

SANDWICHES AND MARMALADE

Sandwiches and marmalade
And chips and peas and toffee!
Eat it up
And drink it down
And have a cup of coffee.

THE GRAND OLD DUKE OF YORK

Oh the grand old duke of York,
He had ten thousand men.
He marched them up to the top of the hill
And he marched them down again.
And when they were up, they were up
And when they were down, they were down
And when they were only half way up,
They were neither up nor down.

GOLDILOCKS AND THE THREE BEARS

ACT ONE

SFX 1 Announcement

SFX 2 Overture

Prologue

> *(Simple Simon enters through the auditorium and makes his way on to the stage in front of tabs).*

Simple Simon

Excuse me. Hold everything. Sorry. Now the theatre manager has asked me to make a few little announcements before the show begins. So... first of all, please don't rustle sweet papers throughout the show as this can be most distracting to others. Oh, and if you have anything to drink please don't make loud slurping noises. *(imitates noise).* Oh yes, and when you find something funny, please laugh, - a ha ha!

> *(conducts response – which is poor).*

Oh my goodness! Give me an a ha ha!

(repeat)

Give me a hee hee hee!

(repeat)

Give me a ho ho ho

(repeat)

and a hoo hoo hoo

(repeat)

yes You You You! and you!

(points to someone)

Oh sorry to wake you up! Now!

(brings things to order and conducts)

Ha Ha Ha! Hee hee hee! Ho Ho Ho! A ha ha ha ha hee hee ha ha ha – huh?

(to himself – clutches forehead)

Oh my goodness. We're gonna need all the help we can get. Oh yes, and can you please make sure all mobile phones are switched off.

(interrupted by sound of mobile phone)

SFX 3 phone ringing

There you are! See – there's always one. Oh it's me!

(realises it is his mobile).

Hello! What do you mean "get on with it"? I'm doing my best.

(to audience)

It's the theatre manager! What? One of the actors isn't feeling well?

(to audience)

One of the actors isn't feeling well. What? Who? Really? How exciting! I'll do my best, sir. Yes I will. I won't let you down. Bye! Bye! Bye!

(puts phone away and starts shaking)

Ladies and gentlemen, boys and girls, for this afternoon's performance the part of Simple Simon will be played by... ME.

(paces up and down)

So what do I do? Yes. I'd better begin the story straight away.

> *(picks up large storybook and begins turning pages).*

Once upon a time there lived a beautiful young girl named Go... Go... Oh dear, this is a long word – Go...

> *(to audience)*

Do you know who it is? Oh, that's right, thank you! A young girl named Goldilocks and she worked with her father in the circus. Would you like to meet her? (Yes)! Would you? (Yes)! Would you? Well let's join the circus with Goldilocks and her father, the Ringmaster as we present "Goldilocks and the Three Bears"!

Scene One - At the Circus

> *(Tabs open. Simon sings 1st verse of a circus song and is then joined by Goldilocks and Ring-master.)*

SFX 4 Circus Song

Goldilocks
Today our travelling circus is going to (name of town) isn't it father?

Ring-master
That's right Goldilocks.

Goldilocks
Is everything all right, father? You sound a bit sad.

Ring-master
I'm afraid the circus doesn't seem to be as popular as it once was Goldilocks.

We're barely taking enough money to pay the bills.

What we need is a new act – to liven up our show. If only we could find something really different – that everyone would enjoy.

Goldilocks
Well father. Perhaps it's lucky we came to *(names place)* today.

Ringmaster
Why's that?

Goldilocks
Because I've heard that three very special, very famous bears are living here.

Ringmaster
Oh yes, that's right!

(with enthusiasm).

Goldilocks
Yes, they're showbiz bears.

Ringmaster
Showbiz bears?

Goldilocks
Yes, they've been in show-business all their lives –
they can sing ...

Ringmaster
They can dance!

Goldilocks
They're funny and cuddly.

Ringmaster
And everybody loves them!

Goldilocks
Yes, their names are Mummy Bear, Daddy Bear... and
Baby Bear.

Ringmaster
He's the extra, extra cuddly one!

Goldilocks

Yes, he's lovely. And father, don't you think they'd make the most wonderful new act for our circus?

Ringmaster

Yes I do. I think they could save our show.

Goldilocks

Would you like to see them boys and girls? Would you?

Ringmaster

Well, they're living here right now.

Goldilocks

Yes in the posh part of town.

Ringmaster

(Says well-chosen local district)

Goldilocks

Well father, let's go and see if we can find their house and ask them if they'd like
a new career – with us!

Ringmaster

Hooray! Oh I love you Goldie. You always make everything right.

(Goldilocks and Ringmaster exit. Enter Baron von Lederhosen in spooky lighting)

SFX 5 Baron Play-on

Baron

(to audience)

Did you hear that? Did you? Well I'm going to put a stop to their silly plans. Oh yes! My name is Baron von Lederhosen. I used to work for the Ring-master and his goody-two-shoes daughter, Goldilocks, in ze circus. But that Goldilocks brat got me ze sack, when she saw me whipping some of ze horrible smelly animals. So now I run a circus of my own. I have lots of money, so I can pay people more than they can. Soon they will have to close their circus down and I will be the winner! Ha ha ha ha ha! You'd much rather see my circus wouldn't you boys and girls? I'm so clever, aren't I? Oh yes you would! Oh yes you would! What? I've never been so insulted. I am the great Baron von Lederhosen. I'll show you. I'll be back! I'll stop Goldilocks... You'll see!

SFX 6 Baron Play-off

(Exit Baron - Enter Simple Simon carrying story-book.)

Simple Simon
Hello! Hello! It's me again boils and germs. Remember? Simon. All my friends call me Simple Simon. No, that's not true. I haven't got any friends

(aah!). I've got less friends than that!   Would you be my friends? Would you? Now if we're going to be friends we should get to know each other. As you know my name is Simon, but I don't know all of your names. So, after three shout out your names. One, two, three.

(shouts from audience)

Brill! Absolutely fabulous! Your name's .....

(imitates shouting).

That's a nice name! I'm just called Simon. I'm always unlucky. Just the other day, I was walking past a building site when a brick fell and missed my shoulder by six inches – it hit me on the head! But it's always good to have friends, and you look like the best friends any guy could have. Hey listen! As you can see I am still carrying the story-book. I have to put it somewhere safe so that we can all keep finding out what happens next. For instance ...

(looks at book)

It says here that we will soon meet the bears. Would you like to see them? Would you? Well it says that Goldilocks will visit their cottage in the woods and a great adventure will unfold. You know when I said I didn't have any friends?

Well, that's not quite true. I do have one special friend. Her name's Goldilocks. Have you seen her? Anyway, I'd better go now. You keep an eye on my book and I'll See you later. Bye!

(Enter Goldilocks)

Goldilocks
Oh what a lovely book. I like stories.

(audience shouts)

Simon
Thanks gang! Oh it's her.

Goldilocks
Simon, you're back.

Simon
No, that's my front, but it's an easy mistake to make.

Goldilocks
You are silly! Simon, why do we have a story book?

Simon
We need this so we can keep checking it to see what happens next.

Goldilocks
Well, we'll leave the book there now and then anybody can look at it if they want to.

Simon

That's a good idea. Then anyone can find out what's happening next if they need too.

Goldilocks

Good! Shouldn't you be working?

Simon

You're quite right. I shouldn't.

Goldilocks

Oh honestly! Why can't you stop being silly for once? There are lots of things that need to be done.

Simon

I can be sensible, Goldilocks, really I can. If people would only trust me to do things.

Goldilocks

Well, in that case Simon, if you want to be trusted, here's what I'd like you to do.

Simon

Oh, anything for you Goldilocks.

Goldilocks

This is all the money we have left. Please put it somewhere safe where no-one can steal it.

Simon
I suppose this means no-body will be paid again this week?

Goldilocks
I'm afraid it does Simon. But I'm sure it won't go on like this for long.

Simon
You can trust me to put this money somewhere safe. I won't let you down, Goldilocks.

(Exit Goldie.)

Simon
(sings to audience)

"Hey baby! Ooh! Aah! Will Goldilocks be my Girl?" Did you see the way she was looking at me? Makes me go all weak at the knees. Now where am I going to put this money? If I can find a really safe place for it, then maybe Goldilocks will stop thinking that I'm silly all the time and see how I feel about her. Oh let me see. A-ha! Brilliant! I'll put it with the story book

(Yawns)

Oh! And now it's time for bed.

(puts on night-cap).

Night-night everybody!

(waves and makes as if to exit)

Night-Night!

(repeats)

Nightie Nightie!

(repeats)

Pyjama Pyjama!

(repeats, then exits – then Baron enters)

SFX 7 Baron Play-on

Baron
Ha ha ha! Tis I, Baron Von Lederhosen the cleverest person in the world! I saw the way Simon and Goldie were looking at each other. They think they might be falling in love – well I'll soon put a stop to that. Oh yes! When I get their circus closed down they won't feel so lovey-dovey then will they boys and girls? Then everyone will have to come to my circus instead and my circus will be the best! Won't it boys and girls? Oh yes it will! Oh yes it will? Bah! Who asked you anyway?

(Exit Baron and Enter Goldie.)

Goldilocks
Hello everyone!

(hello)

Have you seen Simon?

(yes)

Has he gone to bed?

(yes).

Oh dear – he's no use. He shouldn't be going to bed now – there's lots more work to be done. I can't go to sleep. In fact I need waking up so I can keep on helping my father. We've got to look after our circus and keep it going. I know – let's sing a song to keep me awake. Let's do a song with lots of actions. Will you help me? Will you? Let's do my favourite waking up song – all about my uncle – The Grand Old Duke of York. Do you think you can do it with me everybody? Well let's have a practice.

(Goldie teaches audience movements)

SFX 8 Grand Old Duke of York

Goldilocks

Let's have one more go!

SFX 9 Grand Old Duke of York

Goldilocks

Oh that was great! Well done everybody. Now boys and girls, do you know where Simon has put the bag of money? Over here?   Over here? Over here? Oh! On the book. Oh Silly Simon. He really shouldn't have left it there. Now where shall I put it so it will be really safe? I know. I'll put it in this honey jar. No-one would ever think of looking in a honey jar for money. Besides, I don't even know anyone who likes honey.

(She places money in jar).

Now I'm off to finish my work and then see if I can find where those wonderful bears live. Bye-bye boys and girls. Bye-bye!

(Exit Goldie – music as the 3 bears enter)

SFX 10 Bears' Entrance Music

Daddy

Hello everybody! I said hello everybody!

Mummy
I think they're a little bit shy here today. Hello everybody! Oh lovely.

Baby
Look at all the people, mummy! Have they all come to see me?

Mummy
They've come to see all of us dear – because we're famous.

Baby
Why are we famous mummy?

Mummy
Because we can sing and dance.

Daddy
Yes, we're musical bears.

Mummy
Talented bears.

Baby
Modest too!

Daddy
Now, you two, we've come here to look for food, and look what I've found.

Baby

Honey! That's what bears love best! Yum yum!

Mummy

See you later everyone. Bye-bye!

Daddy

Bye bye boys and girls.

<u>SFX 11 Bears' Play-off/ Dame Entrance</u>

> *(Daddy Bear takes the honey-jar and the bears exit. Music as Sarah the Cook enters. She has a Scottish accent.)*

Sarah

Oh yoo hoo! I said Yoo hoo! Oh I don't think you've had the pleasure of me. My name's Sarah the Cook and I work at the Three Bears cottage. I look after their every need! And they're lovely! Have you met the three bears yet? Have you? Well that bonny wee bairn Baby Bear (oh he's so cute), he wanted to play in the woods before breakfast so Mummy Bear and Daddy Bear took him out to play while I made their favourite breakfast for them. Can you guess what it is? No, not kippers. Try again.   No not rice crispies. No, not beans on toast. Oh yes. That's right. How did you guess? Porridge. Scotts porridge oats only the best. I cook all their food for them. I do wonderful recipes and they're very appreciative. Nigella Lawson, eat your heart out. I do choc ice and chips. Mmmm- very scrummy. And I do marmite and ribena sandwiches – Mmmm Yummy. Scrummy tummy! And I do cornflake and beefburger Curry. Mmm. And I do fish finger and ice cream salad. That's my favourite. Now every time you see me, I will call out Yoo-hoo and I want everyone to call back yoo hoo – okay? I tell you what – let's have a wee practice. Right. I'm coming on now. Yoo-hoo – yoo hoo.

(Practise a couple of times)

Oh that's fabulous. I can tell we're going to get on really well. Tell you what, boys and girls! Would you like to help me with my breakfast song? Would you? All you've got to do is repeat everything after me. Are you ready? I'll teach it to you. This is what I have for breakfast every day. Here we go! Sandwiches

(audience repeats... sandwiches)

And marmalade

(and marmalade)

And chips and peas and toffee

(and chips and peas and toffee)

Eat it up

(eat it up)

And drink it down

(and drink it down)

And have a cup of coffee

(slurps)

Mmmm! Now sing it with me, boys and girls. It's a tune you already know

(unrolls words on tree and points with pointer)

(sung to the tune of "Jack and Jill Go Up the

Hill")

SFX 12 Sandwiches and Marmalade

That's very good. Let's try again. Everybody sing!

(this is said over music between verses)
Lead applause at the end.

Oh wonderful! Now do you know what, boys and girls? I think we were having the same problem there that Goldilocks had with her Grand Old Duke of York song. The mums and dads weren't joining in. So if you've got any grown-ups near to you, will you keep a very close eye on them for me? Will you do that? You watch them very carefully and make sure they're singing all the words. Okay? Here we go. All together now.

SFX 13 Sandwiches and Marmalade

(Sarah leads applause)

Oh! Well done! Very good indeed. But I can't stand around here prittle-prattling all day. I'm off to the shops to get a new outfit. I'm looking for something a bit more colourful. I hear there's a sale on at Miss Selfridge and their skirts have come down. I'll see you later. By- bye! Bye-Bye!

SFX 14 Dame Play-off

(Enter Goldilocks and Ringmaster)

Goldilocks
Good Morning father.

Ringmaster
Good Morning Goldilocks. Well, I'm afraid it's not very good news that I've got for you. That nasty Baron von Lederhosen is still following us around. Everywhere we go he appears with his own circus. As a result, not enough people are buying tickets for our Circus and we are losing money. So I'm sorry but I can't afford to pay anyone again this week.

Goldilocks
Is it true that the Baron is cruel to his animals, father? I've heard that he whips them and keeps them in cages.

Ring-master
I'm afraid it is true Goldie.

(Enter Simon dragging weights)

Ring-master
The way to defeat the Baron is to not give in. Soon everyone will find out how nasty he is and won't want to work for him any more.

Goldilocks
Yes, I suppose you're right.

Simon
Hi!

(falls over because weights are too heavy)

Goldilocks
Oh Simon, you don't need to have muscles to impress me. I would much rather have a boyfriend who could use his brain.

Simon
Really?

Goldilocks
Yes! I'll just take those.

> *(takes weights from Simon without any effort at all)*

Ringmaster
Oh Goldilocks, where did you put the money that I gave you last night? Remember I said it was all the money we had left.

Goldilocks
I gave it to Simon. I don't think he is as simple as some people say so I thought this would give him a chance to show how clever he can be.

Ring-master
Oh dear! I'm not sure I like the sound of this.

Simon
Don't worry, Ring-master. I put it in the storybook.

> *(searches)*

Well that's strange! I put the money right here.

> *(points to book, as audience intervenes)*

Ringmaster

I think it's time we looked in the storybook again. Now where are we? Oh! It says that Goldie saw where you'd left the money.

Goldilocks
And thought it wouldn't be safe there.

Simon
(looking over Ringmaster's shoulder)

So she put the money in a honey jar. Oh wonderful. That's where it is then.

Goldilocks
Yes father. The money's safe and sound in the…. Oh no! Where's the honey-pot gone?

Simon
It's gone missing.

Ringmaster
Do you know where the honeypot is boys and girls?

(audience shouts)

Simon
Some bears took it?

Ring-master

Oh this is terrible news. Without that money we will have to close down the circus. Now Goldilocks, my lovely daughter, you know such a lot about animals. Is there any way we could get our money back? And why on earth would bears want to take our money in the first place?

Simon

Well, let's begin with the bare facts of the case. Ha ha! Bare facts, get it?

Ring-master

(Crossly)

That's quite enough from you, young man. You've caused enough trouble already. You were given a chance to prove yourself but it seems that you really are Simple Simon.

Goldilocks

Yes, if you hadn't put the money in such a silly place I wouldn't have found it and put it in the honey jar.

(Goldie throws weights at Simon and he falls backwards off the stage).

I am sure that the bears didn't mean to take our money, father. It must be those famous bears that we've been looking for. You see, bears are active at night-time when they roam around trying to find food

- and their favourite food is honey. They must have taken our honey-jar because they thought it contained honey.

Ring-master
But can we get our money back?

Goldilocks
I'm sure that we can. I will go in search of the bears straight away. Goodbye father! Bye-bye boys and girls. Bye-bye!

> *Goldie and Ringmaster exit. Lights go to black-out, with just a pin-spot on the Ringmaster reading from the story book.*

SFX 15 Play-off/ mood change

Ring-master
And now boys and girls the storybook says.... Goldilocks searched far and wide for the bears' cottage. She knew if she could only find the bears' house she could return the money to her father and she might be able to persuade the talented bears to join the circus. Eventually... she said...

Scene Two – The Bears' Cottage

> *(Back to special lighting on cottage as Goldilocks enters)*

Goldilocks

Oh dear! I'm getting so tired. Wait a minute. I think this might be where the
bears live! Well, here goes. Hello! Hello! Is anybody there? Oh, there's
no answer.

(*she enters cottage).*

Hello? Hello? Oh look! There's bowls of porridge –
and each one is a
different size. Actually I'm quite hungry. I'm sure they wouldn't mind if I tried
some.

(Large bowl).

Oh dear this one is much too hot. (*Medium size bowl)*
And this one is much too
cold.

(Small bowl)

But this one – this one is just right. Oh dear! I seem
to have eaten all of the porridge from the small bowl.
I must have been hungrier than I thought. And
it was so delicious. Oh! Look at these chairs. Again,
they are three different sizes.

(She sits in the large chair).

This one is far too hard.

(medium-size chair)

But this one – this one is much too soft. I wonder who that small chair belongs
to. It looks so tiny. I'm going to try it.

(She sits in the small chair)

Oh! This one is just right.

(She breaks off one of the arms).

Oh dear! Oh no! I've broken it. I feel so tired after all that walking through the woods. I think I had better have a lie down. Night-night everybody. Nightie nightie!

(yawns – sleepily, slowly...)

pyjama....py...ja....

(Enter the three bears who stand together by their bowls).

SFX 16 Bears' Song

Daddy
Who's been eating out of my bowl?

Mummy
And who's been eating out of my bowl?

Baby
And who's been eating out of my bowl, and look, they've eaten it all up.

(Baby bear is comforted by Mummy.)

Daddy
Who's been sitting in my chair?

Mummy
And who's been sitting in my chair?

Baby
And who's been sitting in my chair, and look, they've broken it.

(Baby is comforted by Mummy again.)

Baby
And look, they're still here.

(Goldilocks is heard to give a slight scream and wakes up.)

Goldilocks

Oh dear! Oh goodness! I must have fallen asleep. I'm so sorry!

Mummy

Now, now my dear, you just calm down and tell us what you're doing here.

Daddy

And while you're about it perhaps you can tell us what right you have to wander around in people's homes uninvited. We could call the police, you know.

Baby

Yes, and you've eaten my porridge and broken my chair.

(starts crying)

Goldilocks

Oh dear, I really am sorry . You see, my name is Goldilocks and I've come from Goldie's Circus. My father, the Ring-master, and I discovered that our money was missing and I just wondered if you may have taken it by mistake. It was inside a honey-jar.

(Daddy retrieves honey-jar from behind counter)

Daddy
>*(chuckling)*

Is this what you're looking for!

Goldilocks
Oh yes. That's it.

>*(She takes out the money which is still inside).*

Daddy
Well, I suppose there's no harm done. We were going to return the money tonight, so you've saved us a trip. And don't worry, Baby Bear, we'll make some more porridge and I'll have that chair of yours fixed in no time.

Baby
Cor, thanks Daddy.

>*(Sarah enters. She is carrying shopping bags.)*

Sarah
Yoo-hoo

>*(audience: yoo-hoo) repeat.*

Oh they're quite good here, Mummy bear. See they remembered.

Baby

Much better that that dreadful, useless lot in (nearby town) yesterday.

Mummy

Baby Bear, that's very rude.

Goldilocks

I must say, you really do have a lovely cottage.

Daddy

Thank you, Goldilocks. We are very happy living here. As long as there's room enough for us to rehearse our routines.

Goldilocks

Rehearse? Routines?

Mummy

Yes. Let's show her what we can do Daddy Bear!

Daddy

Yeah!

(*picks up guitar, ready to perform a song*)

Hit it Mr Sound Man!

SFX 17 Bears' Rap

Goldilocks

Wow, I thought I knew a lot about animals but I didn't realise that bears were musical.

Baby

Most bears aren't. But my parents are so cool.

Daddy

That's quite enough, Baby Bear. We don't want you getting over-excited!

Goldilocks

Anyway, I was just wondering if you had ever thought of joining a circus. I'm sure lots of people would pay good money to see performing bears, and then Goldie's Circus would be successful once again.

Sarah

Oh that's a great idea. Oh go on. Say you'll do it. Say you'll do it. I've always dreamt of a career in show business. I'll be your agent!

Mummy

Oh dear, I think Baby's not the only one who's getting over-excited.

Daddy

It sounds like a marvellous idea! We would love to join your circus Goldilocks. And while you're here we'd love to teach you our favourite song.

SFX 18 Bears' Song

Goldilocks

Oh Wonderful! We must go and tell father.

> *(Bears and Goldilocks exit waving and calling "goodbye – see you later").*

Sarah

Oh, I'm so excited.

> *(picks up guitar and strums as she attempts to sing and dance)*

Mmm

> *(studies guitar)*

I think this is a wee bit out of tune. I can't wait to see what happens next though. I'll have a wee look in the book. Now let's see, where are we? Oh yes, Goldilocks found the bears, didn't she?

> *(Turning over pages of book).*

Ah, here we are. The bears decide to join the circus. And then – Oh no! That's terrible.

> *(Gradually change to dim blue lighting)*

Sarah

It says here that the Baron... Oh dear... Oh that's dreadful. I can't read that out. I do hope it will be all right, but you'll have to see for yourselves boys and girls – in part two. See you later! Bye!

(tabs close)

SFX 19 Final Chords/ Announcement

INTERVAL

ACT TWO

SFX 20 Entr'acte/ Announcement

Scene One: At the Circus

SFX 21 Baron play-on

Baron
Yes! It's me! Baron Von Lederhosen again. I know
what that silly girl Mouldy Socks and her father are up
to, but I'll stop them.   I am going to kidnap the three
bears. I'm going to capture them. Then they will be in
my circus and not Goldie's. Ha ha ha ha! That's a
brilliant idea isn't it boys and girls? Bah! Who asked
your opinion anyway?

SFX 22 Baron play-off

(Exit Baron and enter Goldilocks)

Goldilocks
Hello everybody. Have you seen the three bears? I
think they're a little bit late for their rehearsal.
They're meeting me here to practise their new routine
for our circus.

(looks out into wings)

Oh! Wonderful. And here they come now. Ladies and gentlemen, boys and girls the very talented…. Three Bears!

(no-one enters)

Oh? What's that? You want applause for your entrance? Oh very well – I suppose they are stars now. Let's all clap and they'll come on. Please welcome …. The 3 Bears!

(Claps).

Oh? What's that? You want a cheer as well? And a feature in Hello magazine? We'll settle for the clapping and the cheering!

(to audience)

Are you ready? Ladies and gentlemen, boys and girls… the fabulous three Bears!

(Claps and Cheers)

SFX 23 Teddy Bear song

(Bears perform. Goldie joins in)

Goldilocks

Oh wonderful! Well done! You're going to be terrific in our circus. Let's go and tell father all about your new song.

    (Exit Goldie and the 3 bears. Enter Baron carrying a big chain.)

Baron

Did you hear that? Mmmm So did I! And that song has given me an idea ... a chain! What a brilliant way for me to capture those horrible smelly bears. Aren't I clever? Oh yes I am. Oh yes I am! Oh! Sssh! Quiet everyone! The bears are coming back!

SFX 24 Teddy Bear song reprise tag

    (Enter Bears to music of song)

Baby

Oh Mummy, Oh Daddy! I can't wait to do our song on opening night. Do you think anyone famous will be there to review our act?

    (Baron approaches wearing fake moustache))

Baron

Good morning to you all. I've just seen your new song and I've come to help.

Daddy
(suspiciously)

Who are you?

Baron
(camp tone)

I am Peter. Peter Pins and Needles, the theatrical costumier.

Baby
What's a theatrical costumier?

Mummy
That's someone who makes costumes for shows.

Daddy
You'll need to know all these things Baby, if you're going to be in show-business.

Baron
Yes! That's right. I was explaining the very same thing to (current celebrity) only the other day.

Daddy
What do you want anyway?

Baron
Well it's that song. It mentioned a chain. To do the song well – you need a real chain.

Mummy

(to Daddy)

Yes, I suppose he's right. That's very kind of you, Peter.

Baron

Yes, isn't it! I mean – oh no trouble at all. Anyway, here's a lovely chain.

(in Baron's voice)

Put it on!

(holds up chain - then camp voice again)

I mean why don't you try it on? It's such oooh-smooth metal! And the colour is so this season.

Daddy

What do you think boys and girls? Do you think we should try on the chain?

(audience inter-action – all shouting "no!")

Mummy

Why not? What? Well I think Peter's right. It would make a lovely addition to our song.

Daddy

(to audience)

And I think you're all spoil-sports. Peter's just trying to help.

Baron

(Camp)

Yes that's right. Now we just wind it around here... like this.... And then around here..... and a little bit more round here...

(ties up all 3 bears)

There!

(Back to Baron's voice).

Now my silly furry friends – the truth! Tis I,

(tear off moustache – ow!)

Baron Von Lederhosen – the cleverest man in the world! Yes I've trapped you – you silly smelly bears. And now you will be mine!

Bears
Oh no! Please! Never! No!

Baron

Yes! Now you'll work for me and my circus will be the best. Ha ha! Come along my friends. You're going to do what I say now.

Bears

No! Never! Let us out! Help!

Baron

It's no use arguing. There's no escape. You're mine! All mine! Ha ha ha ha!

(Exit Baron pulling bears with chain, then enter Goldilocks)

SFX 25 Baron play-off

Goldilocks

Oh I'm starting to feel a bit confused. I've always thought Simon was so silly –
but now I'm beginning to wonder if there is a bit more to him after all.

SFX 26 Goldie's love song

(Enter Simon carrying flowers prop -5 separate flowers)

Simon

Watcha gang! Hello! Hey gang, can you keep a secret? Can you? Well, you know Goldilocks, right? Well, you see, the thing is

(clasps hands to chest).

Oh she's here! Hello Goldie!

Goldilocks

Hello Simon, I'm very worried about the bears. There's no word from them. Do you know what's happened?

Simon

(with flowers behind his back – very bashful and silly)

Goldilocks, I've got something to tell you.

Goldilocks

About the bears?

Simon

No! I want to tell you I lo... I lo...

(tries to say the word "love", but can't)

Goldilocks

Oh really, Simon don't bother me now. This is very important. Boys and girls, has anything bad happened to the bears? What's that? Oh no, not the

Baron? What has he done? Kidnapped them? This is dreadful. We will have to try to rescue them.

Simon
Erm, Goldilocks?

Goldilocks
What is it Simon?

Simon
I have an important question to ask you. Will you... erm, will you do me the honour of..... that is to say, will you....?

Goldilocks
Oh, really Simon, I'm sure this can wait.   We have an emergency to deal with

>*(Goldilocks exits. Simon calls after her wistfully, but she is gone before he finishes his sentence. Enter Sarah the Cook.)*

SFX 27 Dame play-on

Sarah
Yoo hoo! For me? Oh, you shouldn't have.

>*(Sarah takes flowers and places them in the flower tub)*

What's up Simon? Why so sad?

(She passes him a large hanky which he uses very noisily and hands back).

Er, no, that's okay. You keep it.

(Simon and Sarah stand together. Simon is holding flowers in front of him.)

Simon
I'm having a really bad day, Sarah. Nothing seems to be going right.

Sarah
Well you tell me all about it. I've got a very sensitive side, you know.

Simon
Oh thanks, Sarah. Well, when I got up this morning I found that my hamster had died.

(The first flower wilts)

Sarah
That's terrible. How did he die?

Simon
He fell asleep at the wheel. And that's not all.

Sarah
I feared as much.

Simon

I want Goldilocks to be my girlfriend but I'm too scared to ask her. I don't think she wants me.

(A second flower wilts)

Everyone thinks I'm silly and can't be trusted to do anything.

(A third flower wilts)

And on top of all that, the boys and girls have just told us that the three bears have been captured by Baron von Lederhosen.

> *(Despite the sound cue, the next flower does not wilt. 2 flowers left – neither of them wilts. Simon and Sarah begin to corpse. Simon shakes the flowers. Nothing happens.)*

It worked yesterday.

Sarah

You know what we should do, Simon? We should rescue the bears.

Simon

Yes! We must rescue those bears. We must mount our proud stallions and venture forth. We must fight to the death with honour, majesty and glory.

(Simon acts out his words in a ridiculous manner and then trips up)

Oh, I've hurt me toe!

Sarah
Now listen Simon – we are going to look for the bears and I want you to do exactly what I say. If you see a leopard – shoot it on the spot!   Keep an eye out! Put your shoulder to the wheel! Your nose to the grindstone. Keep a low profile! Have your ear to the ground! And Mums the word!

(Simon acts out all of Sarah's instructions)

Simon
Mummmmmmmmmmmmmmmmmmmmmmmmm!

Sarah
Any questions?

Simon
Yes – how am I supposed to move in this position?

(Sarah turns and sees the ridiculous position Simon is in.)

Sarah
Scram!

SFX 28 Comedy play-off

(Exit Simon & Sarah and enter Ringmaster)

Ringmaster
Oh dear, oh dear. I think something dreadful must have happened. The bears have disappeared and I can't even find Simple Simon or Sarah the Cook

(Chuckles)

I'm not so sorry about Simon, but Sarah was going to cook supper for us all. It was going to be chicken nuggets... *(pause)* pizza.....chips.....baked beans....Coca-Cola......ice cream.......Maltesers......and chocolate milk shake. So you can see why I'm concerned. What's happened boys and girls? What? I'm not sure what you mean. I tell you what. I'll look in the storybook. That'll tell me what's going to happen next.

SFX 29 Mood change

(Goes over to book in pin spot as house is re-set).

Now let me see – we've seen Goldilocks and we've seen her Dad, the ringmaster. Oh yes, of course, that's me! We've seen the bears, and the dreadful Baron – and we've seen funny Sarah the Cook and Simple Simon. But – there's just one person left that we haven't seen yet and that's the wise old crow, who lives on the roof of the 3 Bears cottage. It says here that he always knows what to do and the storybook says that Goldilocks goes to meet him.

Scene Two – The Bears' Cottage
(*Enter Goldie*)

Goldilocks
Oh, I'm so worried about the bears. I hope they're all right. At least I've found their house so I'll just see if they're at home.

Crow
(*Puppet above roof of house*)

They're here but they can't see you.

(*pops down*)

Goldilocks
Who said that?

(*to audience*)

A crow? There's no crow. There's nobody there. Now I wonder if the bears are at home.

Crow

(pops up again)

They're here but you can't see them.

Goldilocks

There it goes again. Somebody's here. Who said that? A crow? There's no crow. There's nobody there.

Crow

It's me!

Goldilocks

It's you?

(To someone in front row).

Crow

No! It's me. Up here. Up on the roof.

Goldilocks

Oh! Hello Mr Crow.

Crow

There's no need to call me Mister. I'm Russell. Russell Crow. Will you introduce me to all the boys and girls?

Goldilocks

Oh yes. Of course I will. You say hello everybody and then they'll all shout back "Hello Russell"!

Crow
Shall we try? Hello everybody.

Goldilocks
Hello Russell. I think they can do better than that.

Crow
Hello everybody.

Goldilocks and audience
Hello Russell!

Crow
Oh lovely.

Goldilocks
Now, Mr Crow – I mean Russell – What did you mean when you said the bears are here, but they can't see me?

Crow
They're being kept here in their own house, but they can't escape. They can't even move. I'm afraid they've been kidnapped and tied up in a chain.

Goldilocks
I know who did that. It was that wicked Baron von Lederhosen. He's always trying to spoil everything for us. What can we do?

Crow

You need to think of a way to trick the Baron. He tricked the bears – now you trick him.

Goldilocks

Oh yes. That's it! You are a wise old bird.

Crow

They don't call me Anne Widdecombe (or current suitable name) for nothing you know. Bye-bye everybody.

(slowly goes down).

Goldilocks

Well I'm sure that was good advice but I really don't know what to do.

(Enter Simon)

Simon

Goldilocks! What are you doing here? Sarah and I have come to rescue the bears. Well, I have. Sarah had to go and cook the ringmaster's tea.

Goldilocks

The Baron's locked the bears in their own home and chained them up. He's going to have them in his own circus and I know they'll hate that. We need to think of a way to trick him.

Simon
What time is it Goldie?

Goldilocks
Ten past seven.

Simon
That's it! The Baron will be coming here to get the bears for his 7.30 performance tonight, and I've got an idea.

Goldilocks
Oh Simon – really?

Simon
Yes! And here he comes now.

> *(Goldie runs to hide behind side of house as Baron enters)*

SFX 30 Baron play-on

Baron
Oh you can't boo me. I am the great Baron Von Lederhosen.

Simon
Excuse me – did you say the great Baron von Lederhosen?

Baron

Yes, that's right.

Simon

Oh, my goodness. I'm so thrilled to meet you. I have always admired you.   I think you're the cleverest person in the world.

Baron

Well yes I am! What a sensible person you are. I'm very pleased to meet you.

Simon

Have I heard correctly that you own some wonderful bears?

Baron

Yes. They're chained up in here.

Simon

Chained?

Baron

Yes. I only untie them for their performances and then I put them straight back in their chains again for the rest of the time.

Simon

You really are very clever – and I'm so glad I met you because I make chains and ropes. I supply them to shipping lines and such like.

Baron
Oh?

Simon
And I'd love you to be the first to benefit from using our new, stronger ropes.

Baron
Really?

Simon
Yes. I've got one here. You see metal chains will cause damage to the bears' skin and fur.

Baron
I don't care about that.

Simon
Yes, but if their fur is damaged they won't look so good in your show.

Baron
Mmmmm. I see.

Simon
Now this new digitally twisted rope is much better. It ties... LIKE THIS!

(Hooks noose over Baron & pins arms to his side).

Baron

Let me go! Let me out of this!

(Goldie reappears from side of house)

Goldilocks

Well done Simon! You really are not so simple after all. You're wonderful! And Baron, you've had a taste of your own medicine.

Baron

Oh I'm sorry. I'm sorry!

Goldilocks

You're not sorry at all.

Baron

I am. Really, I am.

Goldilocks
       (to audience)
Did you hear what he said? D'you think he might be changing his ways?

(audience inter-action)

Simon

Well Baron? Are you?

61

Baron
Might be.

Simon
Well I think you deserve to be punished for all the nasty and mean things you've done. What do you think boys and girls? Do you think we should make him clean the three bears cottage from top to bottom?

Audience
Yes!

Golidlocks
Or should we make him say sorry to each and every one of these boys and girls?

Audience
Yes!

(*Baron goes to front row and starts apologising*)

Simon
No. I know! We should make him eat one of Sarah's puddings.

Baron
Aargh! Anything but that. I'm very sorry. I really am very sorry. This is horrible. I really didn't know how cruel I was being to those bears and all those other animals. This is so painful... just terrible. I really never will hurt any animal or... anyone again. Please

believe me, please. For once I'm telling the truth. I'll do anything. Anything for a second chance.

Goldilocks
You need to start a new life well away from here.

Baron
I will. You see being the wicked Baron wasn't really me anyway.

Goldie and Simon
It wasn't?

Baron
If you'll only let me go I will move away and I'll change my name and start anew.

Goldie and Simon
(to each other)

Shall we?

> *(loosen rope and remove)*

Why   not? We should try to forgive.

Goldilocks
(to Baron)

What's your new name going to be?

Baron

Peter Pins and needles – and I'm going to specialise in theatrical costumes.

Simon

Well you take your chance now and scram before we change our minds! Deal or no deal?

Baron

Deal!

(exit Baron)

<u>SFX 31 Baron play-off (rapid)</u>

Goldilocks

Oh Simon!

Simon

(to audience)

I think now's my moment. I love you more than I can say, Goldilocks. Will you to do me the honour of ... er, that is to say... erm... oh, wait a minute, I've got a present for you.

(Simon rushes over to find flowers)

Goldilocks

Oh, good. I like surprises.

Simon

These are for you.

> *(Then realises he hasn't removed the black cover.)*

Oh! Da-dah!

Goldilocks

Oh, they're lovely!

Simon

Goldilocks, I love you more that I can say. Will you marry me?

Goldilocks

Goodness. Well, this is all a bit sudden. I don't know what to say.

Simon

It's all right, I'll find someone else...

Goldilocks

....except... yes! Oh, where's he gone?

Simon

You don't have to humour me.

Goldilocks

I love you too, Simon and I will marry you.

Simon
I'll be all right. Don't worry about me!

Goldilocks
Simon, I said I love you too and I will marry you - and when father retires I can
think of no-one better to take over as ringmaster than you!

(*They hug.*)

Simon
I'm so happy. I must go and tell everyone the wonderful news. But first, I'm going to untie the bears right away! Bye-bye!

(*goes into house*)

Goldilocks
Bye-bye!

(*enter Sarah*)

Sarah
Yoo hoo! I said, Yoo hoo! Oh marvellous. Now where are the bears? And where's Simon? We were both going to rescue the bears together.

Goldilocks

I know – but you stopped on the way to cook everyone's tea.

Sarah

Well, it was nearly teatime. And in fact, I've got a black belt in cookery. One of my chops and you're dead!

Goldilocks

Sarah, you're too late! Everything's alright now. The bears are safe, the wicked Baron has gone away and, best of all, Simon is going to marry me.

Sarah

Oh Goldie – how wonderful. This calls for a celebration.

Goldilocks

Oh gosh. Not one of your spinach trifles?

Sarah

No! Much better than that.

(to audience)

You've heard of Goldilocks – well today, just for you.... Goldie ROCKS!!

<u>SFX 32 Bears' Rap</u>

Sarah
It has been said that I have one of the best voices in the country. It sounds rubbish in here, but in the country it's marvellous. I think I should have done that other song.

Goldilocks
What's it called?

Sarah
It's about a plumber who says goodbye to his girlfriend. It's called "It's over Flo!"

(Enter bears)

And now, here are the bears safe and well *(leads applause and cheers)* and we can all join the circus.

SFX 33 Circus song (reprise)

SFX 34 Finale walk-down

Goldilocks
(Spoken during middle verse of song)

Ladies and gentlemen, boys and girls, please join me in thanking all my wonderful
friends here today ....

(names all actors as each steps forward for applause.)

Daddy
And as Goldilocks the lovely ....

Goldilocks

Thank you very much. You've been a terrific
audience. You really have.
Now we've got a question for you all – have you had a
good time? I said, have you had a good time?
Wonderful. Now please put your hands together and
give a big round of applause to everyone who works
here at the *(name)* theatre.
They've made us all very welcome here today. And
ladies and gentlemen, boys and girls, so have you. So
until the next time...

All
Goodbye! Bye-bye everybody!

 (all exit, waving)

<u>SFX 35 Final chords</u>

<u>SFX 36 Exit music</u>

THE END

For our wide range of pantomime and drama scripts search authors Derek Grant and Richard Gill.

Pantomime titles available include:
Little Red Riding Hood
The Adventures of Dick Whittington
and his Cat
Humpty Dumpty and the Queen of Hearts Mother
Goose
Goldilocks and the Three Bears
Aladdin

Drama titles include:
Treasure Island
The New Adventures of Pinocchio
The Snow Queen
A Christmas Carol

Printed in Great Britain
by Amazon

42895078R00047